Teddy Bear Towers

Teddy Bear Towers

Story & Pictures by

BRUCE DEGEN

HarperCollins*Publishers*

Teddy Bear Towers
Copyright © 1991 by Bruce Degen
Printed in the U.S.A. All rights reserved.
   2   3   4   5   6   7   8   9   10

Library of Congress Cataloging-in-Publication Data
Degen, Bruce.
   Teddy bear towers / story and pictures by Bruce Degen.
      p.   cm.
   Summary: A boy pretends to be king of an imaginary land of teddy
bears and tries to keep his younger brother out.
   ISBN 0-06-021420-1. — ISBN 0-06-021430-9 (lib. bdg.)
   [1. Teddy bears—Fiction.   2. Play—Fiction.   3. Imagination—
Fiction.   4. Brothers—Fiction.   5. Stories in rhyme.]   I. Title.
PZ8.3.D364Te   1991   90-31937
[E]—dc20   CIP
                                                              AC

Over the ocean
Where sea bears sing
Stands Teddy Bear Towers,
And I am the king.

Tower to tower
And room to room,

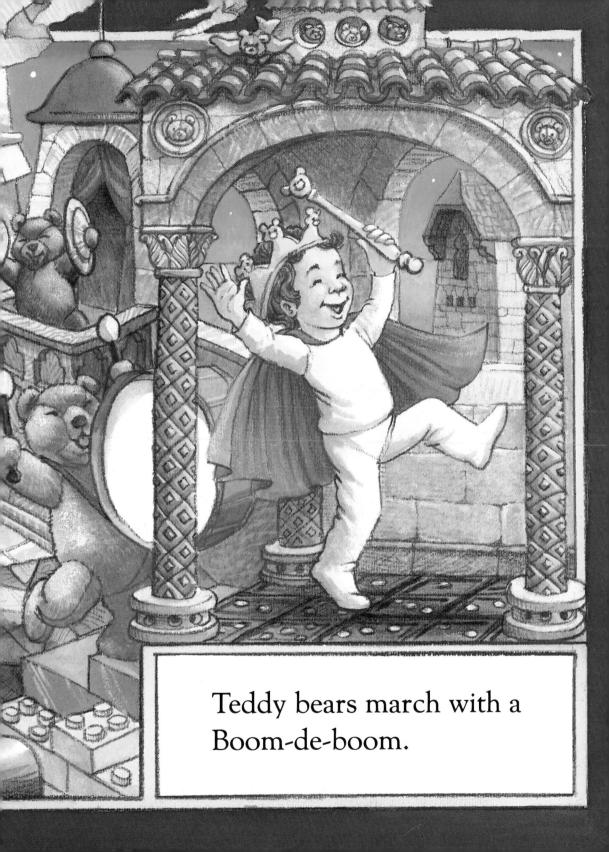

Teddy bears march with a
Boom-de-boom.

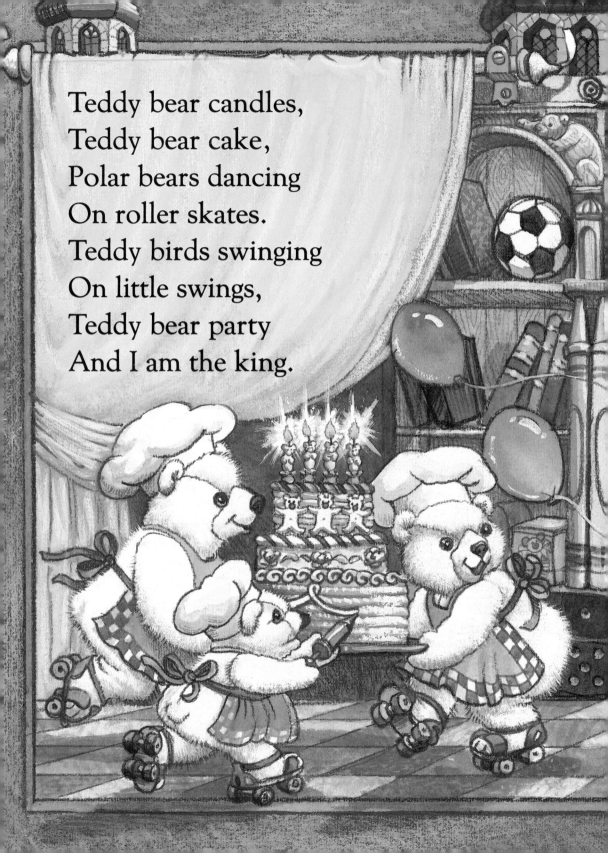

Teddy bear candles,
Teddy bear cake,
Polar bears dancing
On roller skates.
Teddy birds swinging
On little swings,
Teddy bear party
And I am the king.

Who dares to knock?
Who can it be?

Oooh! It's a present!
Must be for me.

Stowaway! Go away!
No one's allowed!
This castle is private.
Two is a crowd.

Teddy bear guards,
Beware! Beware!
Watch from the towers,
Watch from the stairs.
Whether it swims
Or flies or crawls,
Nothing gets over my
Teddy bear walls!

Stop it! Drop it!
Don't you dare!
We're not afraid
Of an old sea bear!

You're pretty tough, kid—
Shake my hand.
I'll let you play
In my teddy bear land.

Over the ocean
Where sea bears sing

You'll be my knight—
but I'm still the king!